Elephany's
Discovery

WRITTEN BY
STACY L. TUCCI-FAUST

ILLUSTRATED BY
ALAN CLARK

About the Author

Stacy lives in McKinney, Texas with her husband Jeremy, daughter Madie and Goldendoodle Winnie. Stacy's hobbies includes baking sourdough and trying new flavor combinations, spending time with friends and family.

AuthorHouse™
1663 Liberty Drive
Bloomington, IN 47403
www.authorhouse.com
Phone: 833-262-8899

Because of the dynamic nature of the Internet, any web addresses or links contained in this book may have changed since publication and may no longer be valid. The views expressed in this work are solely those of the author and do not necessarily reflect the views of the publisher, and the publisher hereby disclaims any responsibility for them.

Any people depicted in stock imagery provided by Getty Images are models, and such images are being used for illustrative purposes only. Certain stock imagery © Getty Images.

This book is printed on acid-free paper.

ISBN: 979-8-8230-3600-9 (sc)
ISBN: 979-8-8230-3602-3 (hc)
ISBN: 979-8-8230-3601-6 (e)

Library of Congress Control Number: 2024921775

Print information available on the last page.

Published by AuthorHouse 11/05/2024

authorHOUSE®

Ephany was walking along a path in the jungle feeling very sad and gloomy, even though it was a beautiful, warm, and sunny day.

1

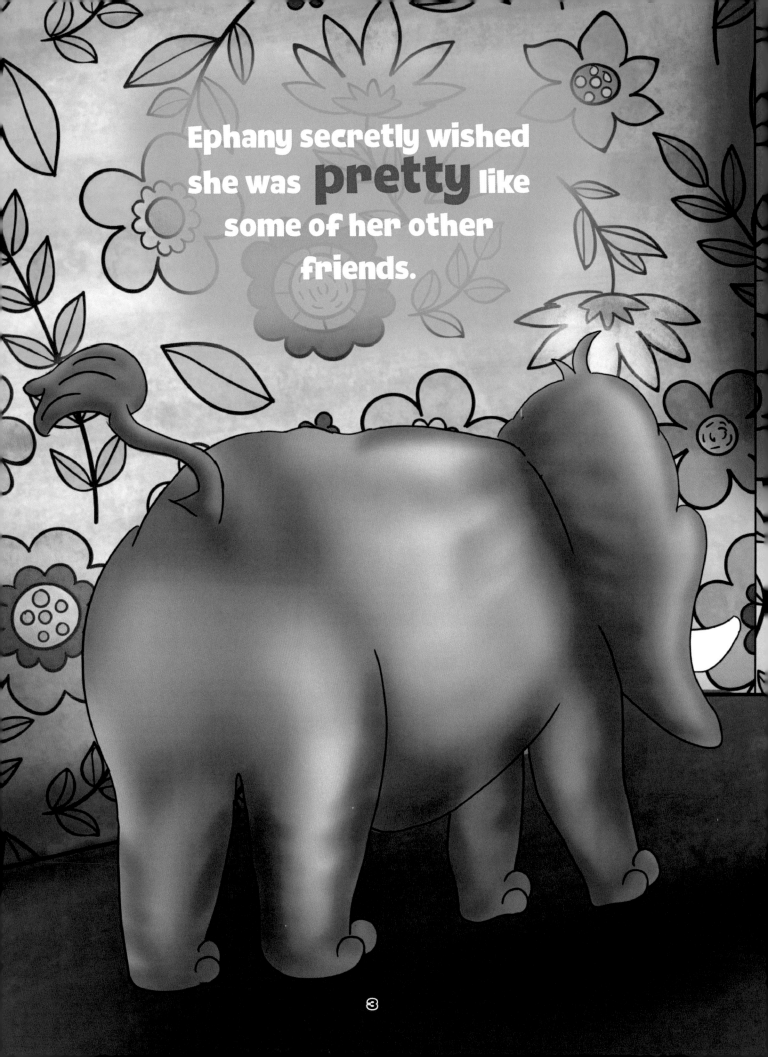

Ephany secretly wished she was **pretty** like some of her other friends.

3

When Ephany looks in the **mirror**, all she sees staring back at her is a boring elephant with a broken tusk. She often wondered if anyone would ever find her pretty.

Ephany was lost in her thoughts as Stanley slithered alongside her.

"Good aft--er--noon Eph---any," he said with a lisp, "How are you to---day?"

"I'm fine," she said, but lowered her head unintentionally.

6

Stanley coiled himself up so that he was almost eye level with her and said, "You don't look fine swee——tie," and asked if she wanted to talk about it.

She replied, "Well, there are so many **beautiful** creatures in the jungle, like yourself, and I wish I was one of them.

8

Eph---any darling you are ador---able. What are you even say---ing right now?"

She replied, "Look at your beautiful markings on your skin compared to, well," **she looked** at her leg as to "show me."

Stanley rose to her eye level and lifted her head up with his head, and he told her that she is **beautiful** and that she is being too hard on herself. She wrapped her trunk around his neck and **hugged him.**

Stanley is a good **friend**, but he wouldn't understand. She told him she must go but will see him later. They exchanged **goodbyes.**

12

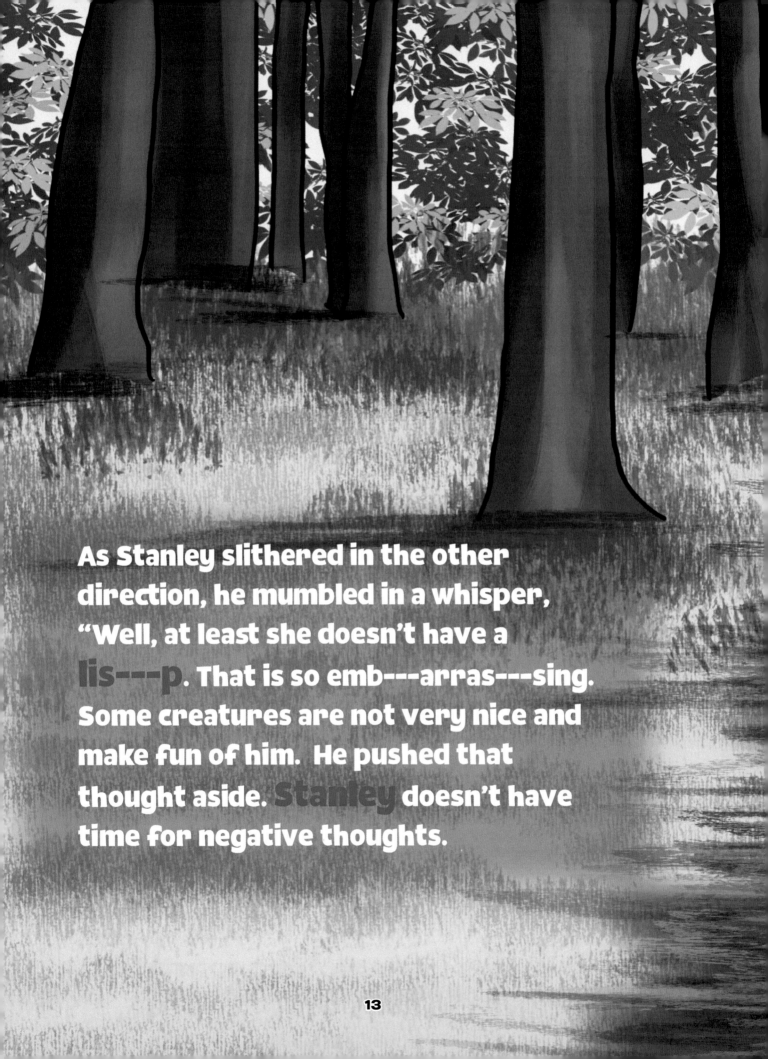

As Stanley slithered in the other direction, he mumbled in a whisper, "Well, at least she doesn't have a lis---p. That is so emb---arras---sing. Some creatures are not very nice and make fun of him. He pushed that thought aside. Stanley doesn't have time for negative thoughts.

He has too much to do today. Ephany has always been sweet and never made fun of him. They have been **friends** a long time and he thinks how lucky he is to have her in his life. They always have a fun time together, as he smiled to himself.

As Ephany walked away from Stanley, she imagined herself with all his beautiful, colorful markings and a cute fedora hat. She busted out laughing at the thought and startled some birds in a nearby tree. That made her laugh even more.

16

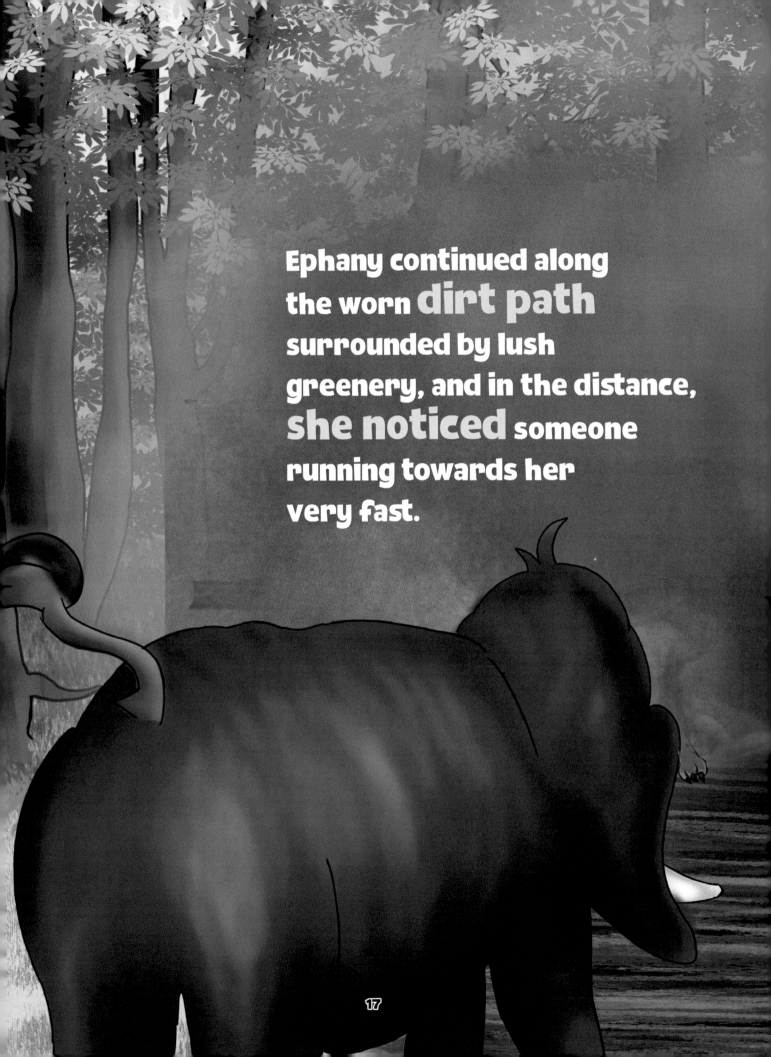

Ephany continued along the worn **dirt path** surrounded by lush greenery, and in the distance, **she noticed** someone running towards her very fast.

She could not make out who it was. A cloud of **dust came** bellowing up as this creature came to a screeching **halt right** in front of her.

The two of them swatted the dust away from their faces and Ephany heard, "Howdy Ephany!" Before the dust could settle, she knew it was her good friend Cora.

Ephany coughed a little with a laugh and said, "Coming in hot sweetie", and smiled.

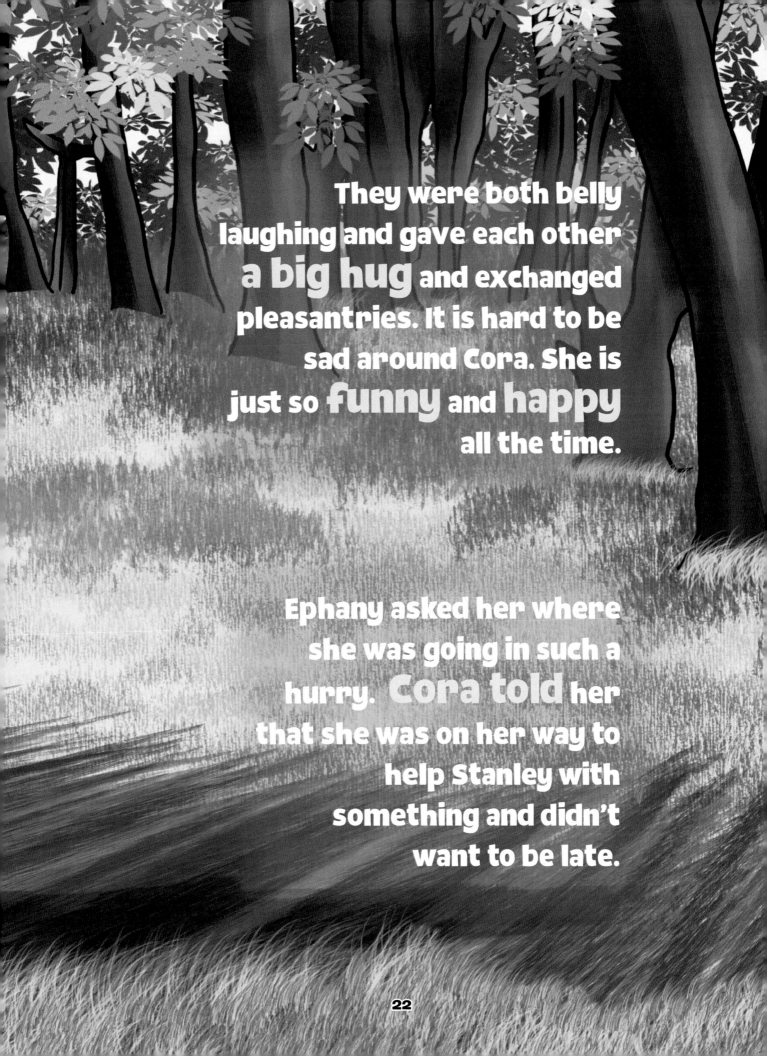

They were both belly laughing and gave each other **a big hug** and exchanged pleasantries. It is hard to be sad around Cora. She is just so **funny** and **happy** all the time.

Ephany asked her where she was going in such a hurry. **Cora told** her that she was on her way to help Stanley with something and didn't want to be late.

"What are you up to today?" Cora asked. Ephany isn't going anywhere special. She smiled and told her friend that she is out taking a stroll, but in her mind added, and to clear my head.

She knew Cora would want to talk about what's in her head if she mentioned it. She did not want to keep Cora from helping Stanley.

24

Cora told her that they will get together later to hang out and **shouted back**, "Have a great day!" before she ran off.

Before Ephany could finish saying **goodbye**, Cora was gone.

Cora loves to run. She feels so free, plus no one can see her **awful scar** when she zips past them. She tries not to think about the accident she had when she was a cub. Those aren't very good **memories**.

Instead, she thinks about Ephany and how she is such an **amazing friend**. Come to think of it, Ephany has never asked Cora about her scar, or how she got it. **Cora** wondered if she thought it was too ugly to mention.

Cora is always there for her friends when they need her, and she is so adorable. Ephany thinks this to herself as she walks up to the **shallow stream** just off to the right of the lush path. She set her trunk in the cool clear water and took a long drink. She noticed her **reflection** and sighed.

She thought about Cora's **beautiful** orange coat and black spots and imagined **herself** with them. She chuckled at the thought and continued to walk through the **cool water** to the other side.

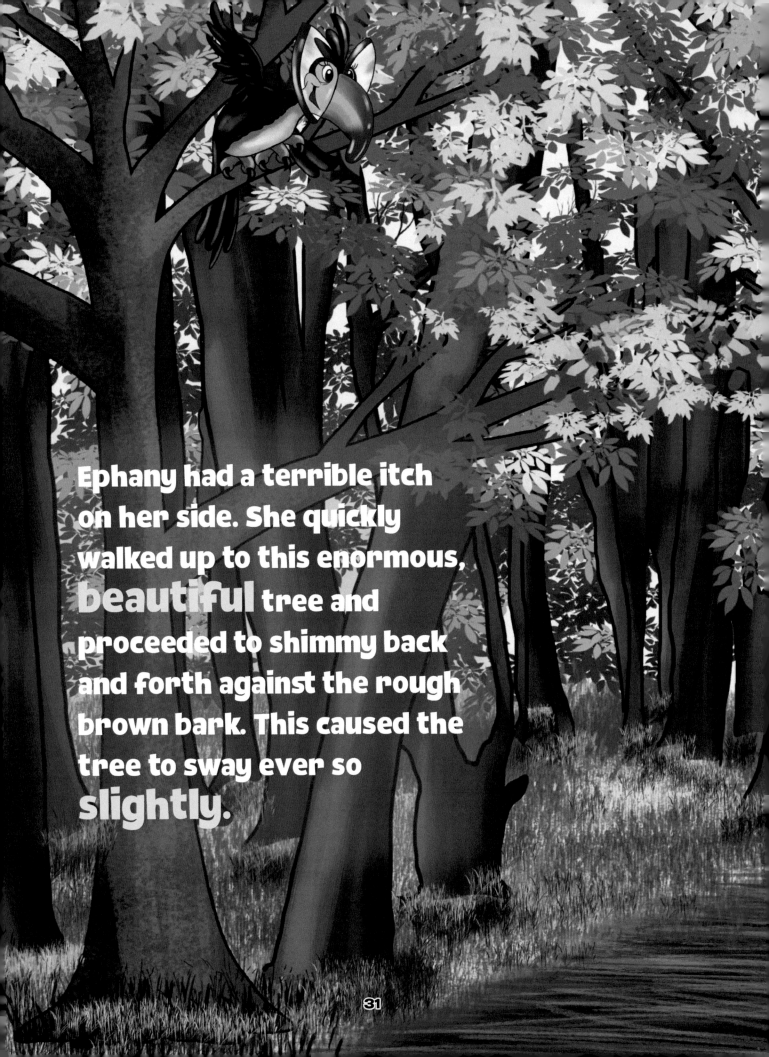

Ephany had a terrible itch on her side. She quickly walked up to this enormous, **beautiful** tree and proceeded to shimmy back and forth against the rough brown bark. This caused the tree to sway ever so **slightly.**

"Oh, that feels good," she said out loud without realizing it. "Hey Ephany," she heard from above. She looked up and saw Tessa sitting on a branch. "Hey, Tessa," said Ephany as she peered up at her friend.

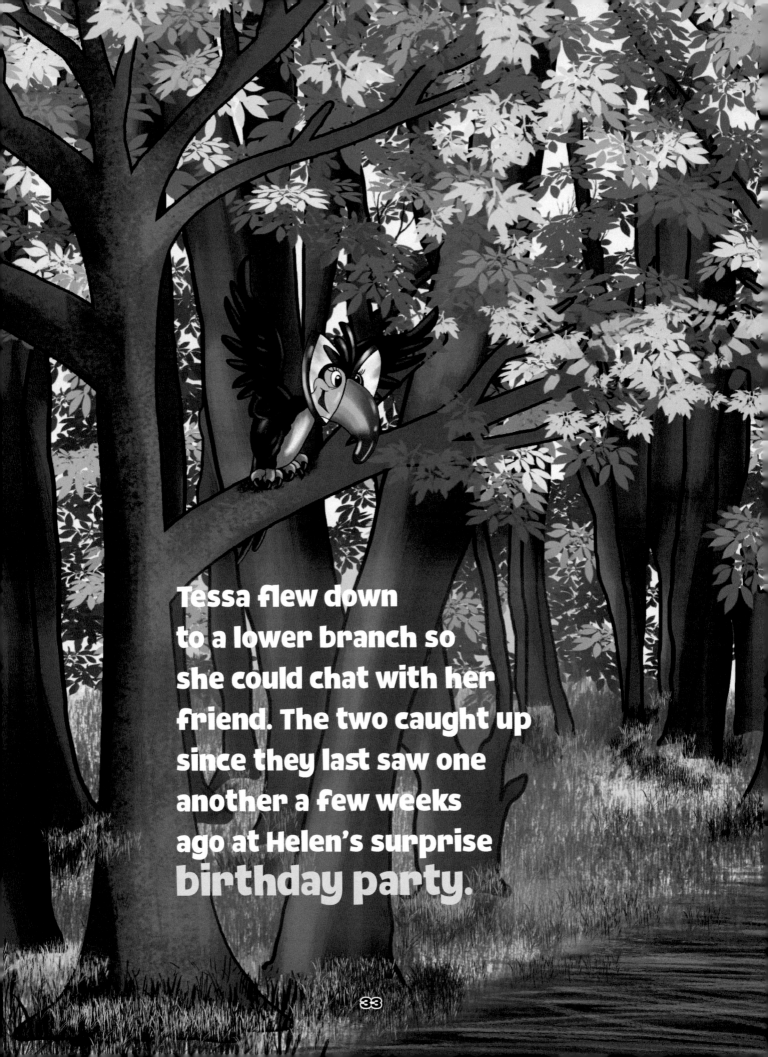

Tessa flew down to a lower branch so she could chat with her friend. The two caught up since they last saw one another a few weeks ago at Helen's surprise **birthday party.**

What a terrific time they all had and how happy they were that Helen was so surprised.

34

Tessa noticed something seemed to be bothering her best friend. "What's the matter?" Tessa asked. Ephany replied, "Oh nothing.

Tessa knows her best friend very well and can tell when she is not being truthful with her, so she pressed her to share. Ephany let out a loud sigh and said, I wish I was as colorful as you are Tessa.

36

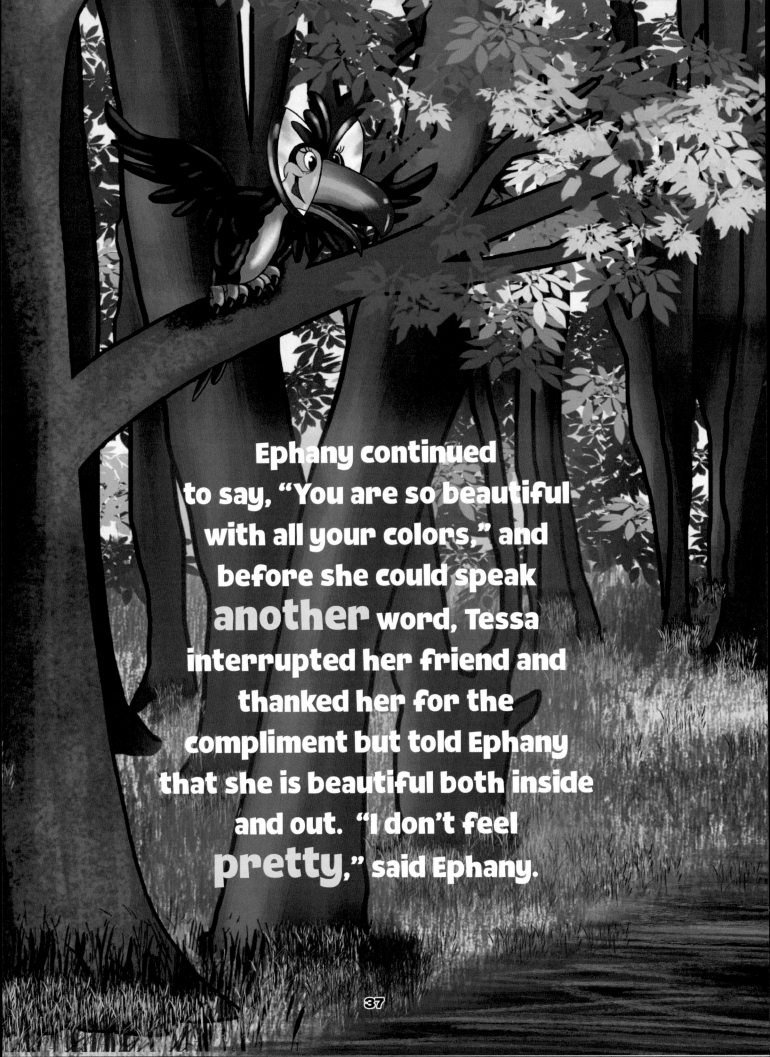

Ephany continued
to say, "You are so beautiful
with all your colors," and
before she could speak
another word, Tessa
interrupted her friend and
thanked her for the
compliment but told Ephany
that she is beautiful both inside
and out. "I don't feel
pretty," said Ephany.

"Look at you and now look at me. You have all these beautiful colors, and I am gray and boring." Tessa told her to lift her head up high. Ephany, you are an amazing friend. You are kind, sweet and thoughtful. Not to mention, look at those big beautiful blue eyes and amazing smile.

Tessa continued to tell her how blessed they are to have her in their lives. "You are **beautiful** inside and out so stop being silly and cheer up.

39

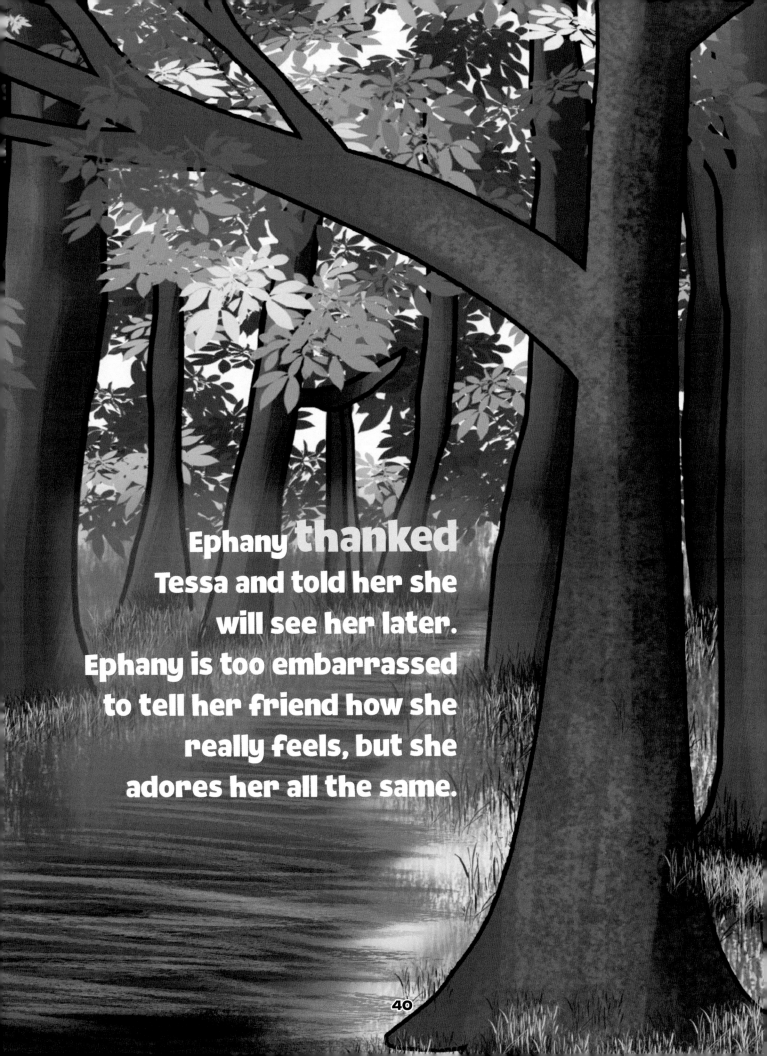

Ephany **thanked** Tessa and told her she will see her later. Ephany is too embarrassed to tell her friend how she really feels, but she adores her all the same.

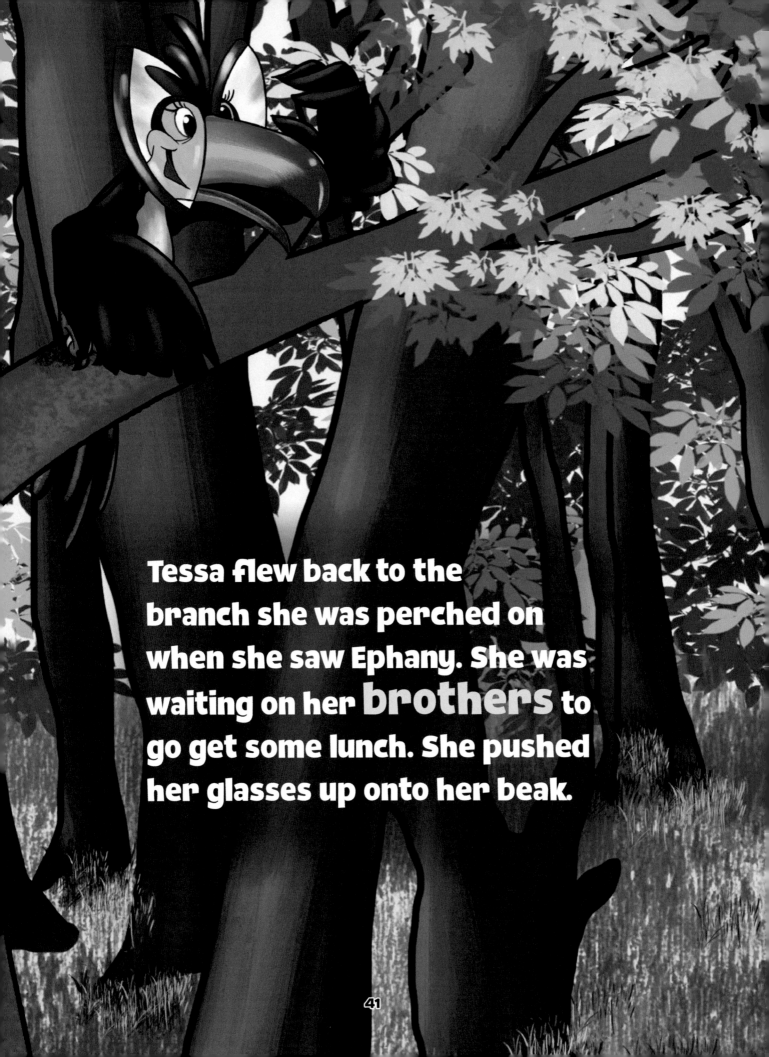

Tessa flew back to the branch she was perched on when she saw Ephany. She was waiting on her **brothers** to go get some lunch. She pushed her glasses up onto her beak.

41

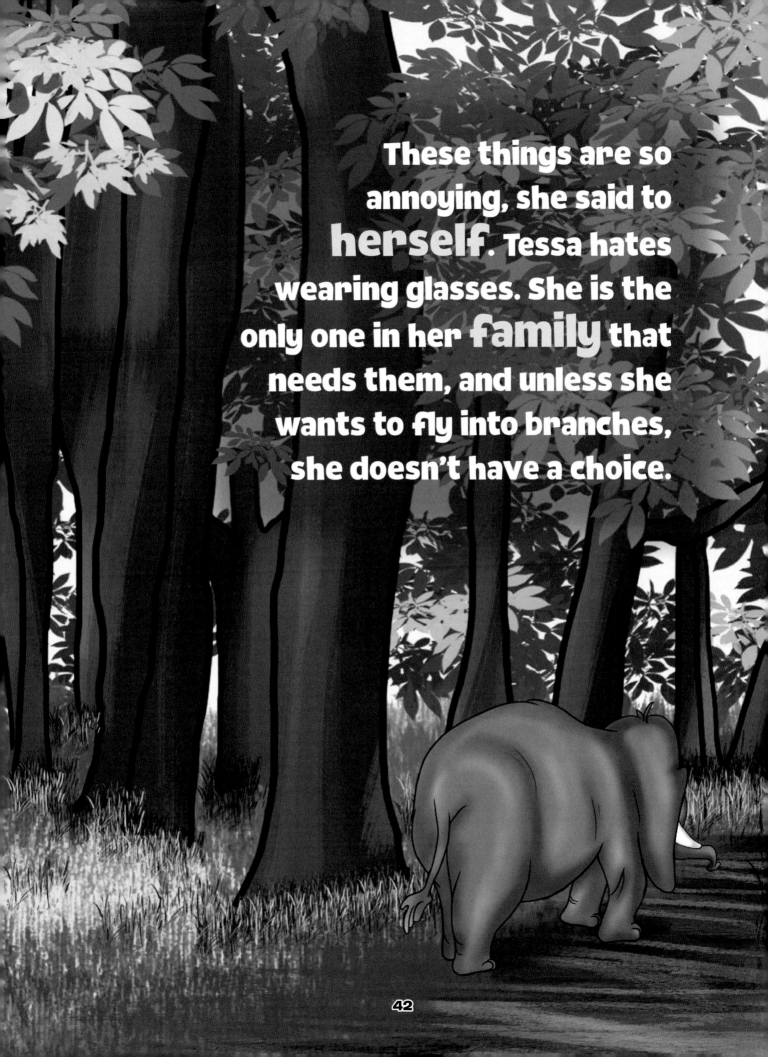

These things are so annoying, she said to **herself**. Tessa hates wearing glasses. She is the only one in her **family** that needs them, and unless she wants to fly into branches, she doesn't have a choice.

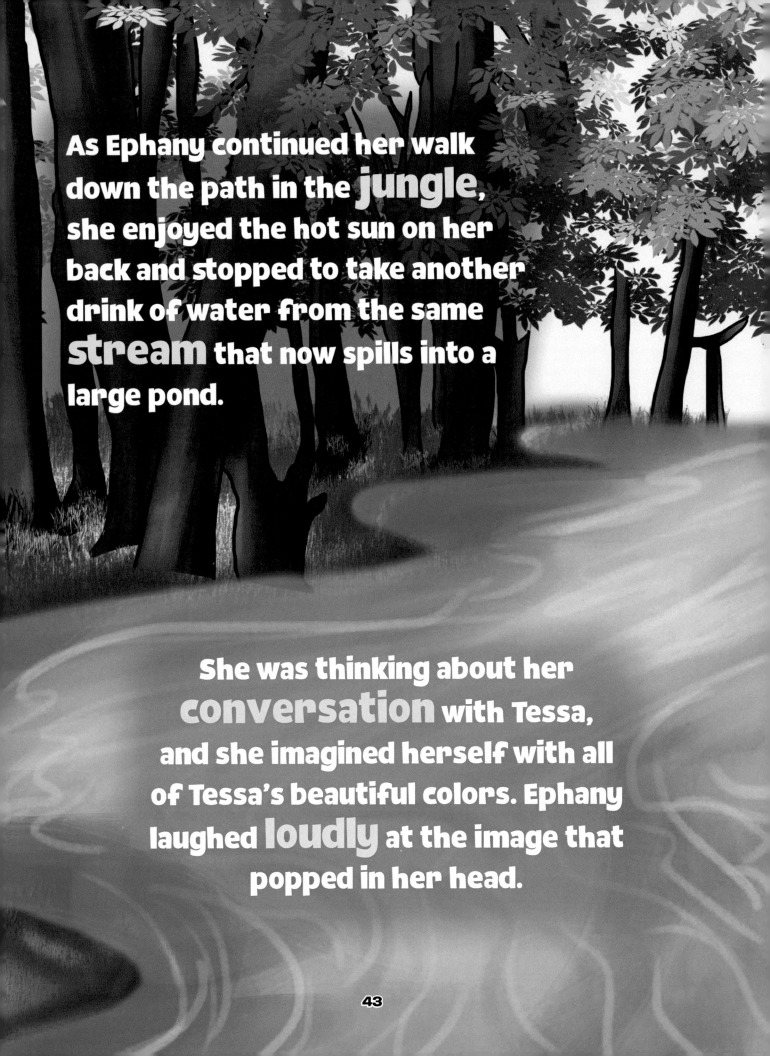

As Ephany continued her walk down the path in the jungle, she enjoyed the hot sun on her back and stopped to take another drink of water from the same stream that now spills into a large pond.

She was thinking about her conversation with Tessa, and she imagined herself with all of Tessa's beautiful colors. Ephany laughed loudly at the image that popped in her head.

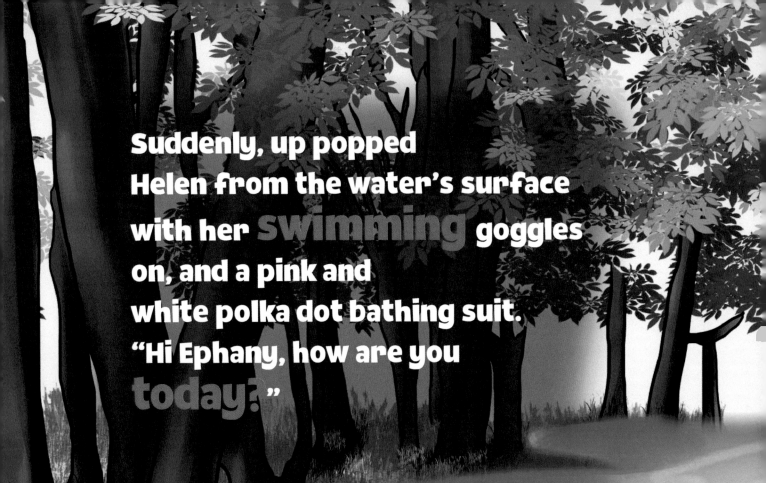

Suddenly, up popped
Helen from the water's surface
with her **swimming** goggles
on, and a pink and
white polka dot bathing suit.
"Hi Ephany, how are you
today?"

"I'm ok, and you?" asked Ephany. "I am fantastic! It is a great day to be **alive**." She asked Helen why today is so great.

Helen, looked around and pushed her goggles to the top of her head, and said, "Isn't the weather beautiful? And just listen to all those birds singing.

Not to mention my good friend is now standing in front of me," she smiled so big, it revealed two very large buck teeth.

48

She quickly reduced her smile to a grin, self-consciously and proceeded to thank Ephany again for her amazing surprise birthday party.

Ephany told her she is most welcome, and she is so happy that she had a wonderful time.

They started sharing stories about the party and laughing about the memories they will always share. Ephany was thinking to herself as they were chatting how beautiful Helen is, although she would **disagree** with that because she isn't like other hippos. She is albino and wasn't born with any **color** pigment on her skin.

Ephany thinks, between her beautiful shimmering pale white skin, the cute freckles that littered her nose and cheeks, and those long bushy white eye lashes that flutter as she talks,

she doesn't realize how stunning she is and how I envy those eye lashes. Just look at them!

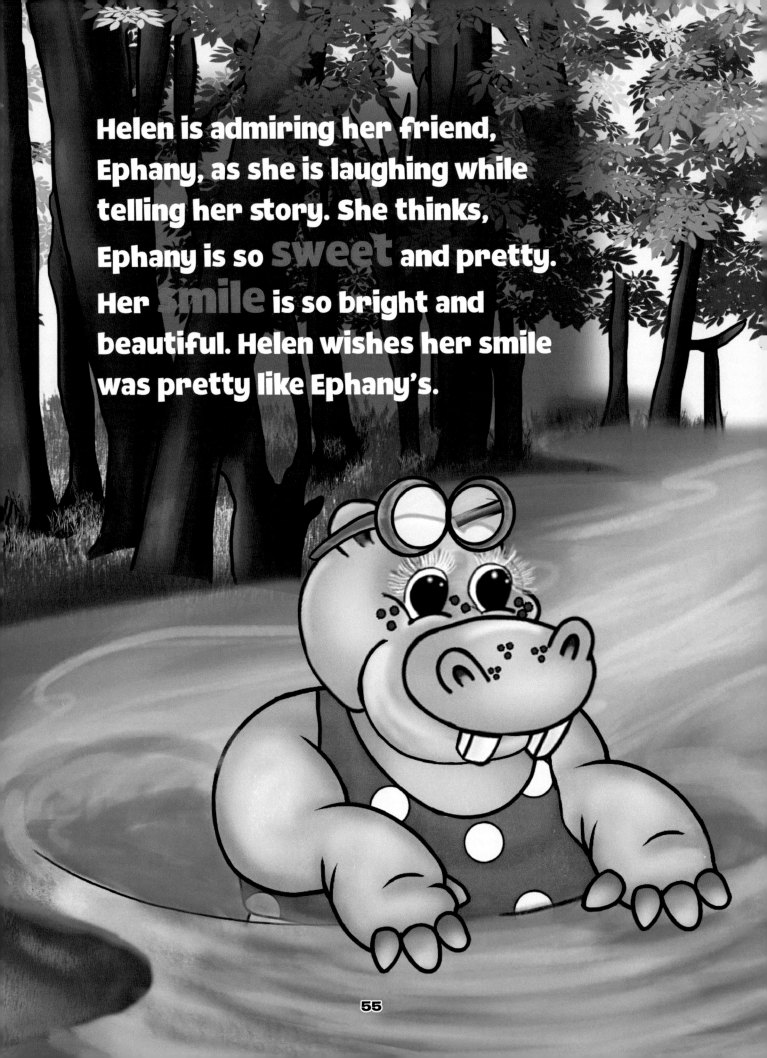

Helen is admiring her friend, Ephany, as she is laughing while telling her story. She thinks, Ephany is so sweet and pretty. Her smile is so bright and beautiful. Helen wishes her smile was pretty like Ephany's.

Helen has always felt shy and embarrassed to smile because of her **big buck** teeth. She thinks they make her look funny.

They both **chatted** a little while longer and then Helen told Ephany she needed to get going and that she **loved** catching up and hopes to see her soon.

Helen disappeared under the **water** and Ephany had an image pop into her head with Helen's **bushy** white eye lashes. She giggled at the thought as she continued along the path.

Along came Penelope hopping out of the thick forest while **constantly** flopping her head back and forth to avoid stepping on her long, floppy **ears.**

Oh, how she hates her ears. She is always **stepping** on them.

Penelope stopped when she saw Ephany on the path. "Hey girl!" Penelope yelled. "Hey Penelope," Ephany responded with a smile. Penelope hugged Ephany's leg as best she could.

She has very little arms when compared to the size of Ephany's leg.

Ephany thinks to herself how cute she is with her long **floppy** ears. She then imagined herself with long floppy ears like Penelope and snorted out **loud**. Penelope looked at her puzzled. "What's so **funny?**", she asked. "Oh, that tickled a bit," and let out a giggle. She didn't want to make her friend feel uncomfortable.

"We **missed** you at Helen's party," Ephany said. Penelope responded that she was **sorry** she had to miss it too.

65

Her sister was having her **babies** and she pulled out a picture of the bunnies and they both squealed with delight at the picture. They are so **fluffy** and cute. As they were fawning all over the babies, along came Al, slowly walking up to them dressed in his signature suspenders, **seersucker** hat, and the plaid scarf he got for Christmas last year.

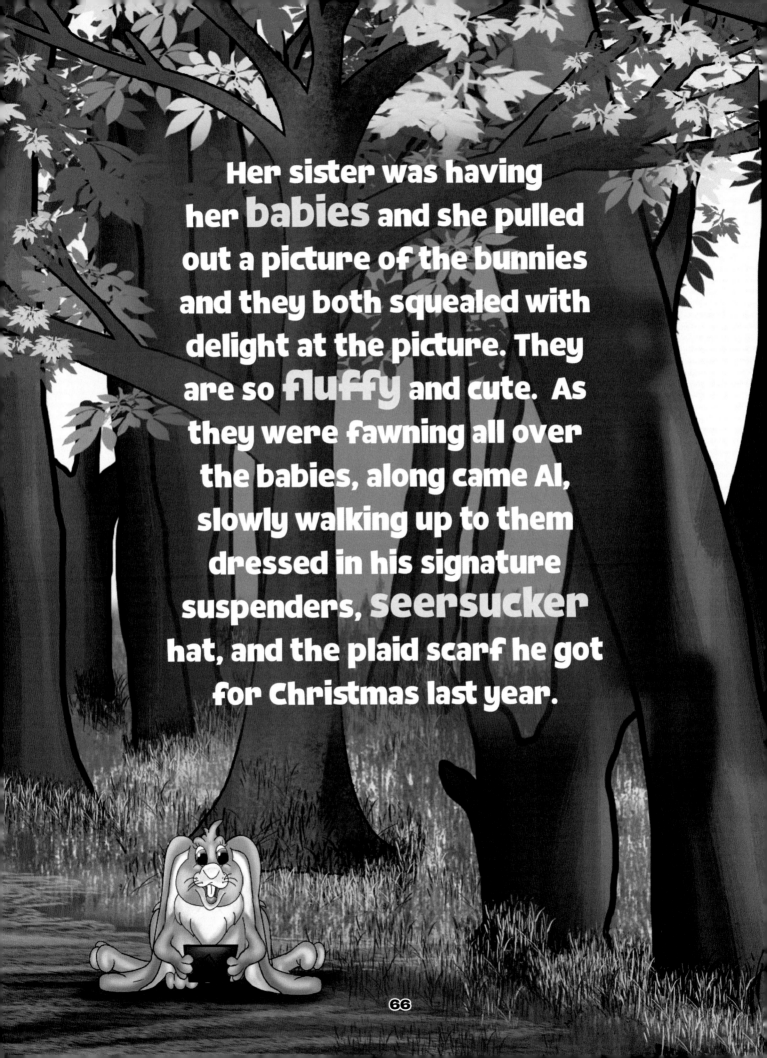

"Hi Al," both girls say to him, **cheerfully**. "How are you today?" Al responded that he is okay but proceeded to tell them about all his aches and pains.

Today his backside is giving him the most **trouble** and he turned his neck to point to the area as to show them the pain that isn't visible. Ephany asks him if there is anything she can do to help, and he **replied,** "Sadly there is not." He reminded them that getting old isn't fun sometimes.

Al asked what they were looking at and Penelope proudly showed him her new nieces and nephews. "Adorable," he said to her. They all caught up a bit and after a while Penelope said she must hop, and Al replied, him too.

Then he added, "Well I won't technically hop away like Penelope, but you know what I mean." They all laughed and said goodbye.

Al shuffled off to his meeting and thought about Ephany and Penelope. How cute are they! Al admired their **friendship**. It reminded him of his own childhood friends. He wondered about them from time to time since they lost touch after they graduated high **school**. Each promised to stay in touch, but we all get busy and time flies by.

He should **look** them up and see what they are up to. He nodded to himself and made a **mental** note to do that when he has time.

73

Ephany enjoyed running into her **friends** Penelope and Al. Penelope is so adorable and Al's **colors** are so pretty, Ephany thought.

A vision of her with Penelope's long **ears** and Al's colors appeared in her mind and she **laughed** at the image. She does have an active imagination, she thought.

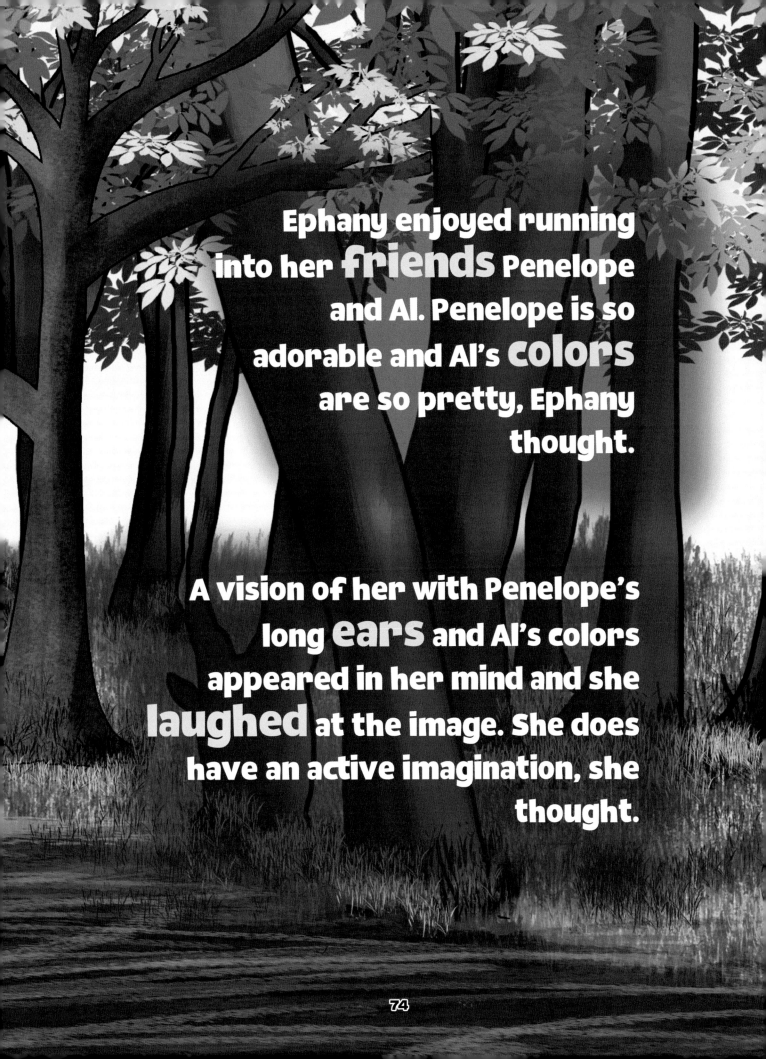

As Ephany rounded the path, she saw the most beautiful creature she had ever seen. "Hello." "Hello," this new creature responded. "My name is Ephany," and "I'm Paisley."

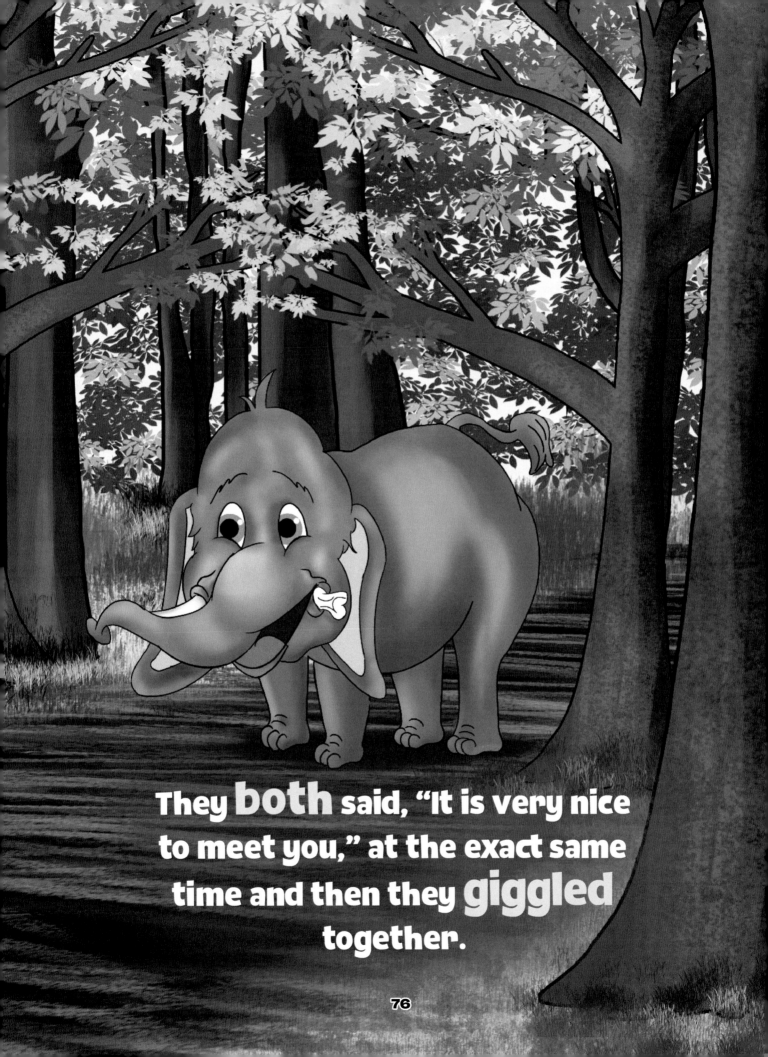

They **both** said, "It is very nice to meet you," at the exact same time and then they **giggled** together.

Ephany is in awe of Paisley and her colors and cannot look away. "You are so **beautiful**," said Ephany. "Why thank you," said Paisley. "If you don't mind me **asking,** what are you?"

I am a Peacock," said Paisley, proudly. Ephany had never seen a peacock before.

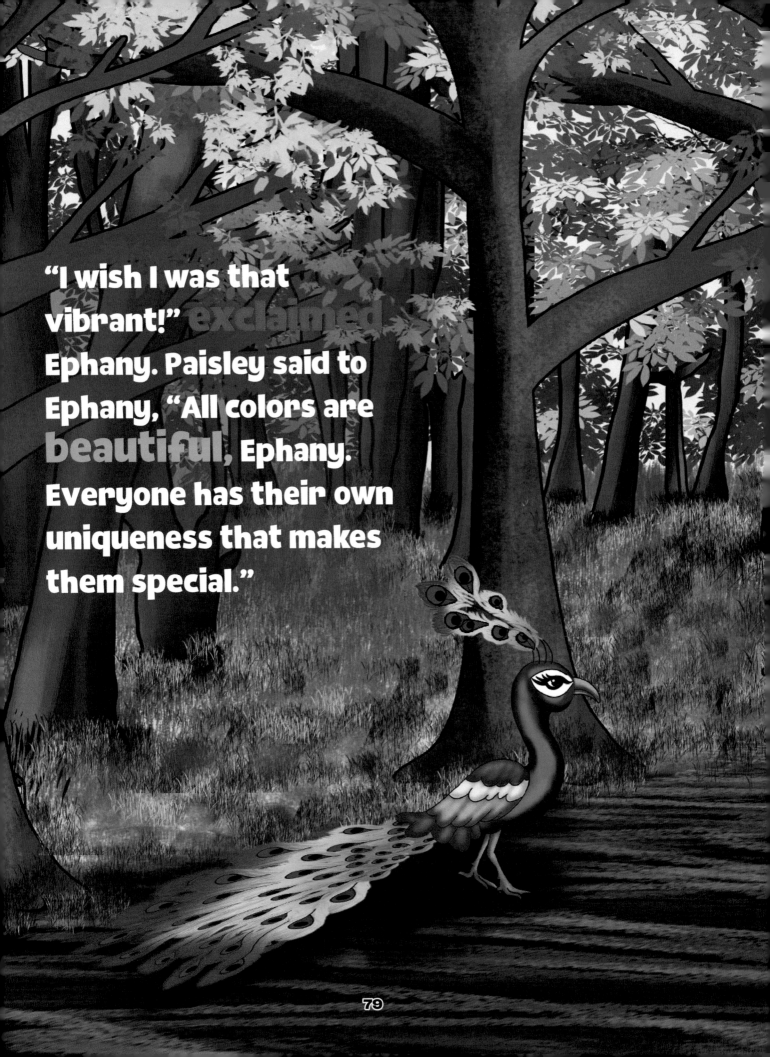

"I wish I was that vibrant!" exclaimed Ephany. Paisley said to Ephany, "All colors are beautiful, Ephany. Everyone has their own uniqueness that makes them special."

Ephany shuffled her feet and said, "Well, compared to all my friends, and you, I'm not very colorful, or pretty."

"Hogwash!" Paisley exclaimed and proceeded to explain that although we are all different on the outside, it is what is in our hearts that truly makes one beautiful.

"If anyone tells you different, than that's not a true friend."

She continued to ask Ephany to think about each one of her friends. Ephany's face lit up as all her friends **faces** came to her mind.

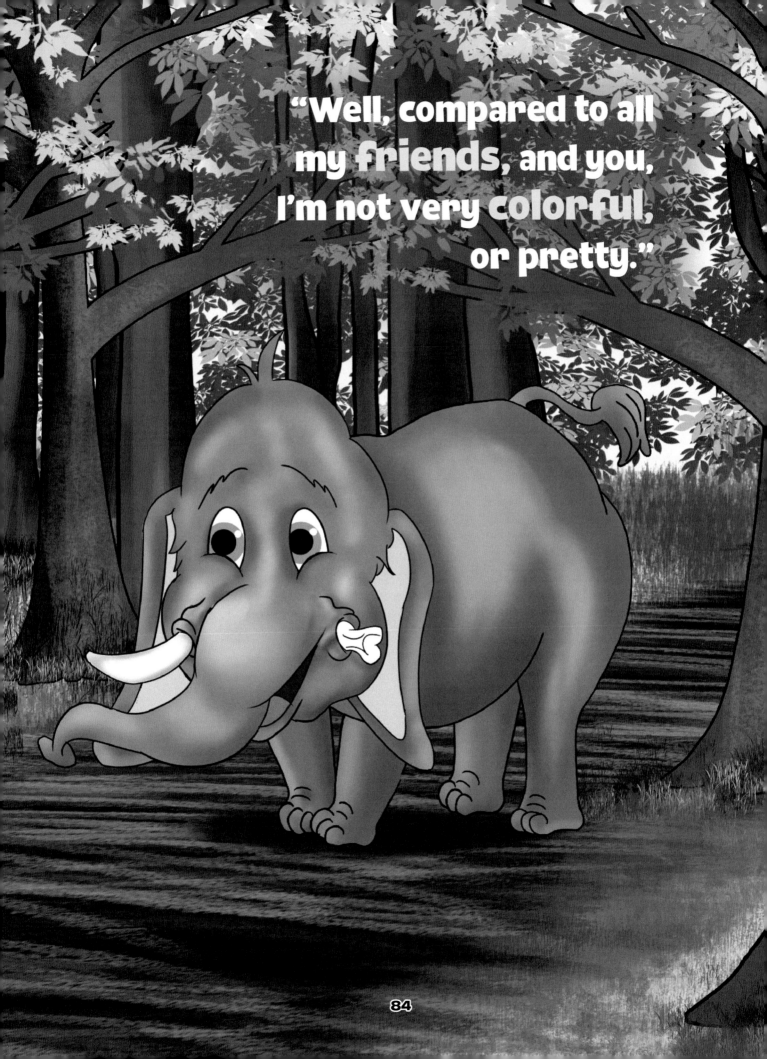

Ephany told her that each one of her friends is **unique** and beautiful in their very own way. Paisley pointed out that she's positive that all her friends feel the very **same** way about her.

Ephany **never** thought
about it like that.

This revelation made
Ephany smile so big it spanned
ear to ear as she realized she
is beautiful in her own unique
way. She stood up straight,
raised her trunk, and let
out a trumpet.

Paisley **laughed** and was so happy that she was able to make her new friend feel so special today. She just knows they will be best **friends** forever.

They both exchanged numbers and **promised** to get together real soon. As Ephany walked up to the waterhole, she **thought** about her day and all her friends she ran into along her path. She realized how **blessed** she is to have all of them in her life.

She thought about each one of her friends and their **conversations** and realized that love and acceptance isn't about what is on the **outside**, but who we are on the inside. That made Ephany very happy.

The End

"Don't be afraid of being different, be afraid of being the same as everyone else."
- Author Unknown

"When in doubt, always choose love."
- Author Unknown

"Be yourself. Everyone else is taken."
- Author Unknown

Printed in the United States
by Baker & Taylor Publisher Services